This book belongs to

_____

_____

For Ada, and my three pals Alex, Finn and Johnny – L.R.

For my family: Jayne, Thomas and Joseph – J.M.

Kelpies is an imprint of Floris Books. First published in 2016 by Floris Books. Fifth printing 2018
Text © 2016 Lynne Rickards. Illustrations © 2016 Jon Mitchell. Lynne Rickards and Jon Mitchell assert their right under
the Copyright, Designs and Patent Act 1988 to be identified as the Author and Illustrator of this Work. All rights reserved
No part of this publication may be reproduced without the prior permission of Floris Books, Edinburgh www.florisbooks.co.uk
The publisher acknowledges subsidy from Creative Scotland towards the publication of this volume British Library CIP
Data available. ISBN 978-178250-255-5. Printed in China through Imago

Skye the Puffling

Lynne Rickards
& Jon Mitchell

Picture
Kelpies

One sunny spring day on a cliff by the sea,
there hatched a young puffling as sweet as can be.

Harris and Isla were bursting with pride.
Their little grey bundle of joy had arrived.

Skye was her name, and she soon let them know
that this cute little fluff-ball was raring to go!

Skye was a lively wee thing from day one.
She had a huge appetite, second to none.

She wouldn't stay still – there was so much to see!
She just couldn't wait to be off flying free.

She'd trip and she'd tumble, and sometimes fall flat.
But Skye the adventurer didn't mind that!

One bright early morning, Skye opened her eyes.
She flapped her short wings and stretched up to the skies.

Both Harris and Isla were still fast asleep,
so Skye tiptoed past them, not making a peep.

The sunrise was lovely, all pink, gold and blue,
and Skye scampered off to admire the view.

She bounced up the cliff and then raced to the top.
She got to the edge – but just couldn't stop!

Over the cliff and then down, down she fell.
She fluttered and tumbled, and let out a yell.

Then, suddenly – *WUMP!* – Skye was on something white...
the feathery back of a gannet in flight!

He lifted her up as he flew through the air.
The gannet had not even noticed her there!

Skye held on tight as the gannet flew on,
beating his wings in the bright morning dawn.

He dipped to the left and she rolled like a ball,
straight down his wing; was she going to fall?

Just as poor Skye felt quite sure that she might,
he turned one more time and she rolled to the right.

Skye grabbed his back and held on for dear life.
This gannet was slicing the air like a knife!

Harris and Isla woke just after dawn,
and that's when they noticed their puffling was gone.

They searched high and low but she couldn't be found.
"Have you seen our Skye? She is small, grey and round."

A seagull swooped down and said, "I saw her, yes!
She's riding a gannet, due south I would guess."

"Let's go!" shouted Harris. "There's no time to lose!
We've got to get out and start looking for clues!"

Isla and Harris zoomed off through the air.
They had to find Skye right this minute – but where?

Harris tried asking some ducks on a beach.
Had they seen a puffling as soft as a peach?

Isla swooped low when she spotted an otter.
Perhaps he'd seen little Skye fall in the water?

"A gannet would fly to Bass Rock," he replied.
"You're right. That's one place we still haven't tried."

While they were searching, Skye still held on tight,
hoping and praying with all of her might.

The gannet looked down, and then dropped like a stone!
She clung to his tail by her wingtips alone.

He zoomed like a rocket straight into the sea,
to catch a big beak full of fish for his tea.

Skye was left fluttering down in a spin.
Big waves rose to meet her – and then she fell in!

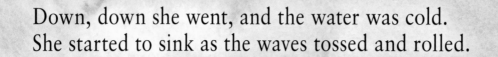

Down, down she went, and the water was cold.
She started to sink as the waves tossed and rolled.

She turned in slow motion, and opened her eyes.
Bright fish darted past her, some three times her size!

More gannets were diving – the fish thrashed about.
Skye kicked her feet hard to try and get out.

The brave little bird reached the surface at last!
She paddled and kicked and she spluttered and gasped.

Then up popped her gannet with fish in his beak.
He swallowed them quickly in order to speak.

"My goodness!" he said. "Come, climb onto my wing.
What's brought you so far from your home, little thing?"

"You carried me here on your back," Skye replied.
"I've been on a very long piggy-back ride!"

"Quick, hold on tight," said the gannet. "Let's fly!"
He got her to safety – a rock high and dry.

Bass Rock was crowded with very big birds.
Their squawking and screeching was too loud for words.

The noise was atrocious. The rock was a mess!
The smell of that white stuff was just as you'd guess.

Skye tried not to worry. She knew she was tough.
But what would she do if that wasn't enough?

Meanwhile, her parents flew on, side by side.
They scanned the horizon and searched far and wide.

A craggy white rock slowly came into sight.
"We've made it – Bass Rock!" they both cried with delight.

The gannets and gulls were soon filling the skies,
But one tiny puffling caught Isla's sharp eyes.

Skye was so pleased when her parents swooped down.
They snuggled her close. "Our dear puffling is found!"

Now, Skye was too small to go back all that way,
so Harris and Isla decided to stay.

All summer, Bass Rock was a playground for Skye.
But autumn was coming – she'd soon have to fly!

Her friends helped her practise to get big and strong.
She flapped her short wings and went running along.

Skye's fuzzy grey baby fluff wore away too.
Her lovely sleek feathers were shiny and new.

One late summer's day, Skye looked out at the sea.
She knew it was time to be grown up and free.

Her parents flew first, after hugging her tight,
then Skye flapped her wings for her first solo flight.

She rose in the air by the light of the moon,
and called to her gannet friends, "Bye! See you soon!"

A life of adventure was waiting for Skye.
She couldn't be happier, now she could fly.